cai
c
books   plans

Nina
Fairy Ballerina
series.

Nicola Slater lives in the north of
England with Dave the cat. Her work can be
seen on books and tablecloths around
the globe.

D0656948

Nina
Fairy Ballerina
series

Nina
Fairy Ballerina

Dream Treat

Anna Wilson

Illustrated by Nicola Slater

MACMILLAN CHILDREN'S BOOKS

First published 2007 by Macmillan Children's Books
a division of Macmillan Publishers Limited
20 New Wharf Road, London N1 9RR
Basingstoke and Oxford
www.panmacmillan.com

Associated companies throughout the world

ISBN: 978-0-330-44780-5

1 3 5 7 9 8 6 4 2

A CIP catalogue record for this book is available from
the British Library.

Typeset by Nigel Hazle
Printed and bound in Great Britain by Mackays of Chatham plc, Kent

*For "The Girls", with love
and thanks for all your support –
here's to our Dream Treat
on the slopes!*

✗✗✗

Chapter One

ina, Peri and Bella were feeling nervous as they made their way to the Second-Years' ballet studio. They were on their way to meet their new teacher, and they were worried they might not like her.

"Let's look on the bright side," said Nina, sounding braver than she felt. "No one can be as bad as Monsieur Choux."

Monsieur Choux was a very strict teacher who had worked the fairies far too hard and had exhausted them.

Luckily Madame Dupré had asked him to leave.

"I hope you're right, Nina," said Peri anxiously.

"Yeah," Bella agreed, shoving her hairclips into place as she flew. "He was a right slug!"

Madame Dupré was in the studio, waiting to introduce the new teacher. She looked on with amusement as Nina, Bella and Peri tumbled in, giggling.

"It's nice to see some happy faces," she said. "But settle down now, please, fairies. I would like you to meet your new teacher, Miss Petunia Bliss."

The headmistress twirled round and gestured to another fairy, who was waiting on the stage behind her.

What a romantic name! At least she doesn't *sound* strict, thought Nina with relief.

The new teacher smiled: a little dimple appeared on each cheek. She gave a curtsey. The class curtseyed back and said, "Good morning, Miss Bliss." Nina noticed how pretty the fairy was. Her hair and clothes suggested she might be fun – she had black curly hair that was swept back from her forehead in a wide, bright pink hairband. Stray curls were kept in place with funky hairclips rather like Bella's, except that Miss Bliss's shimmered with all the colours of the rainbow. Her leotard and wand

were silver, and her tutu was a splash of
rainbow colours too.

"Hi, everyone," said
Miss Bliss. Her voice
was chirpy and
friendly. "You'll
never believe it,
but I was a pupil
here once myself,
not long ago! Your
old teacher, Miss
Tremula, and
Madame
Dupré taught me
everything
I know."
Madame shook her
head, smiling, and
said, "Really, Miss
Bliss, you are very
kind. Fairies, I can see that
your new teacher is too modest to tell
you this herself – up until quite recently

she has been performing with the Royal Fairy Ballet at Clover Garden."

Clover Garden! Nina thought. It's my dream to go there . . .

Miss Bliss cut in quickly, "I was only in the corps de ballet, Madame. I wasn't a soloist—"

Madame held up her wand to protest. "A performance is nothing without the corps de ballet. And now, fairies, I shall leave you to show Miss Bliss what a talented bunch *you* are!" she added, her eyes twinkling. Then she flew back to her office.

The class immediately lined up eagerly at the barre and stood with lovely straight backs, just as Miss Tremula had taught them.

"That's great!" said Miss Bliss approvingly. "I can see you're all raring to go, but before we start, I need to know your names." She pointed her silver wand at the class and sang out:

Silver needle, get to work,
Sew name tags nice and neat.
I can't remember people's names —
You'll have to help me cheat!

A fine glittery thread of rainbow silk wove its way from Miss Bliss's wand over to Nina.

"Oh!" Nina cried. A tiny silver needle had begin threading in and out of her crossover cardigan, sewing her name in beautiful rainbow embroidery silk

The whole class was soon chattering delightedly as each ballerina inspected her own rainbow name badge. What other tricks could this teacher be hiding under her wings?

Once the class had settled down, Miss Bliss asked them if they had any questions. Everyone shuffled shyly and looked at the floor.

Suddenly Bella blurted out, "Why did you leave the Royal Fairy Ballet?"

Now it was Miss Bliss's turn to look shy and uncomfortable. Her face went red.

"I don't think that is any of your business, young fairy," she said quietly.

"But you asked if we had any quest—" Bella protested.

"Let's get on with the lesson then, shall we?" Miss Bliss went on hurriedly, and she flew to the front of the room and began taking the class through a warm-up.

Chapter Two

Luckily Miss Bliss cheered up once she saw how keen her pupils were, and the first lesson turned out to be great fun. After the warm-up, Miss Bliss told the class she wanted to teach them some mime.

"Sometimes a dancer has to communicate thoughts or emotions or even a conversation to the audience. But of course she mustn't speak, so she uses mime. For example, what do you think this means?" Miss Bliss suddenly looked horrified and, crouching down, she turned

her head quickly away from her pupils.
She held up her hands as if she were
pushing something from her.

"Oh, I know!" said Peri, shooting
her hand into the air. Miss Bliss checked
Peri's name badge and smiled. "OK, Peri.
Fire away."

"I think it means you're scared," Peri
said.

"That's right!" Miss Bliss nodded.
"What about this?" she added. She leaned
to one side and bent her left leg while
stretching out her right. Then she turned
her head to the left and put her hand up
to her ear.

"You're listening!" Nina cried.

"Correct!" Miss Bliss laughed. "Now,
I want you all to have a go at miming
to each other."

"But, Miss," said Nyssa Bean, one
of Nina's classmates, "how do we know
which moves to use?"

"We'll get on to that later," Miss Bliss

assured her. "I just want you to have fun for now."

The class divided into groups. Nina, Bella and Peri started discussing what they could do in their mime, but Miss Bliss called out, "Fairies, not a word, please! Miming only!"

Nina shrugged at her friends as if to say, "Better do what she says."

Miss Bliss jumped up on to the tips of her toes and clapped her hands. "That's a great mime, Nina!"

Peri smiled and pointed at Nina, then

she clapped her hands too, to show that
she agreed with the teacher. Nina replied
with a low curtsey to thank her friend for
the compliment. Then Bella decided to
pretend she was jealous of the attention
Nina was getting. She crossed her arms in
an exaggeratedly angry pose and stomped
off, frowning.

"Well done, fairies!" said Miss Bliss.

Peri was enjoying herself enormously.
She hurried over to the grumpy Bella
and put her arm around her as if to
say, "Cheer up." Nina then jumped up
and down, waving, to try to get Peri's
attention again. Unfortunately, she
jumped too high in her enthusiasm, and
lost her balance on the way back down.
She fell forward violently and slapped
Bella with one of her flailing hands by
mistake. Poor Bella was knocked flying
and landed in a heap.

"Ouch!" she cried, rubbing her sore
cheek, which had gone quite red.

"Fairies!" Miss Bliss cried, fluttering over. "What *is* going on? I asked you not to make a sound."

"Yeah, well, try keeping quiet when your friend whacks you round the face," said Bella sulkily.

Miss Bliss laughed. "Up you get, Bella. I think it's time we moved on before we all end up in the Sickbay. Now, I want us to do some work on my favourite ballet, *The Nutcracker*. Mime is used here to help tell the story: for example, when Hans-Peter is released from the spell that turned him into a nutcracker, he shows the Sugar Plum Fairy how Clara killed the Mouse King," the new teacher explained.

Everyone looked at her blankly.

"What's up?" the teacher asked, looking round at the puzzled faces.

"Er . . . who are Hans-Peter and Clara and the Mouse King?" asked Nina.

Bella joined in. "Yeah, Miss. We've

never seen *The Nutcracker*. We don't know what you're talking about," she said.

Miss Bliss looked as shocked as if Bella had announced she didn't know what first position was. "You — you've never *seen* it?" she stammered.

"No, Miss," the class chorused.

"Well, we'll have to see about that," said Miss Bliss firmly. And quick as a dragonfly, she zipped out of the studio.

The class was puzzled.

"Where's she gone?"

"What have we done?"

"Is she cross?"

They didn't have to wait long for an answer. Miss Bliss was soon back, beaming with pleasure.

"It's all sorted!" she cried breathlessly, pushing stray curls back into her hairband as she spoke. "Madame has agreed — I am going to take you to a performance of *The Nutcracker* by the Royal Fairy Ballet in Clover Garden at the end of term!"

Chapter Three

After this exciting announcement, the fairies could think about nothing else. Nina was determined to find out as much as she could about *The Nutcracker*, and at the end of the day she rushed to the library to borrow a Daisy Disc of the music. She flew back to her room on Charlock corridor at top speed to listen to it on her Daisy Discplayer in peace and quiet.

What beautiful music! Nina thought happily as she lay back on her bunk bed with her headphones on. The ballet was

introduced by violins playing a jaunty
tune, and then a silvery flute and soft
clarinet piped up in reply. Nina closed her
eyes and imagined herself pirouetting in a
satin dress on the stage at Clover Garden.

The music faded and a soothing voice
began to tell the story of the ballet. It
was strange and dreamy, and the music
was magical.

How could Miss Bliss have given up
the chance to perform this enchanting
ballet at the Royal Fairy Opera House?
Nina wondered.

Nina's dreams that night were full
of sparkling images of Christmas trees,
dancing snowflakes and a dainty Sugar
Plum Fairy and Prince from the story on
the disc.

She awoke full of energy and
enthusiasm for the term that lay ahead
and decided to get to class early so
that she could ask her new teacher all
about life in the Royal Fairy Ballet.

She finished her breakfast just as her friends arrived in the Refectory. As she approached the Second-Years' studio, she heard some music she recognized drifting down the corridor.

That's the "Waltz of the Flowers" from *The Nutcracker*, she thought.

She hummed along softly to herself as she crept up to the door of the studio and peeped in. What a beautiful sight – Miss Bliss was dancing to the music! The new teacher was so graceful. Every movement

she made was as light as thistledown. As
the music quickened and the percussion
joined in, Miss Bliss whirled faster and
faster until Nina felt dizzy watching her.
The music ended in a fanfare of brass
and the tinkling of a triangle in the
background, and Miss Bliss curtseyed low
to an imaginary audience. When she
looked up she had tears in her eyes – but
then she saw Nina. Her jaw dropped with
shock and she lost her balance.

The teacher quickly stood up straight
and brushed the tears away. She took a
deep breath and said, "Oh, it's you! Hi,
Nina," in a falsely cheery voice. "Sorry,
I was miles away. You're early aren't
you?"

"I, er, yeah . . ." Nina stuttered.

"Don't worry. You haven't interrupted
anything. I was just warming up for the
day," Miss Bliss said carelessly.

Nina swallowed. "Erm, I wanted to
ask you something . . . I was listening to

a disc of *The Nutcracker* last night," she began.

Miss Bliss smiled. "And?"

"Well, I hope you don't mind me asking, but – why did you really leave the Royal Fairy Ballet, Miss?" she asked hurriedly, going bright red in the face.

Miss Bliss frowned, and Nina immediately regretted her question. She turned to leave, but Miss Bliss sat down at the piano and patted the space next to her. "Come and sit with me and I'll tell you," she said kindly.

Nina went to join her.

"The simple fact is, I had too many injuries while I was in the corps de ballet," said the teacher, looking sadly into the distance. "Of course, every dancer hurts themselves at some point in their career, and there are fantastic fairy doctors that can help. But magic can only do so much. One day a ballerina has to ask herself the difficult question: 'Has the time come to give up performing?'"

Nina gasped. "But that's awful! Why couldn't the doctors help you any more?"

Miss Bliss smiled weakly. "Oh, it wasn't the doctors' fault," she said. "Fairy magic can heal broken bones and make them as good as new. The thing is, when a ballerina falls, she doesn't just let herself down, but all the other dancers too. It's your *pride* that gets hurt in the end, and that's much harder to heal. I lost my confidence, Nina," she explained, spreading her hands out. "I talked myself into believing that I couldn't dance well any more. Then the more I worried about falling, the more I fell."

"But you should have talked to someone about it!" Nina cried.

Miss Bliss shook her head. "I did the right thing, Nina," she insisted. "I knew I had to stop performing. But don't look so sad — my story has a happy ending,

you know! I'm over the moon to be here.
I always wanted to be a teacher some
day. That day just came sooner than I
thought."

Nina wasn't sure she believed her. "So
why were you upset just now?" she asked.

"I suppose it's going to be strange to
take you all to see *The Nutcracker*, that's
all. We'll be watching all my old friends
performing," Miss Bliss answered.

"But it was your idea to take us!"
Nina reminded her.

Miss Bliss laughed. "I know, I know!
But that's because you absolutely *must* see
a professional ballet if you want to be a
performer yourself one day. Just because
I didn't make it doesn't mean *you* won't.
I wouldn't be a good teacher if I didn't
give you something to aim for! And I've
already heard such marvellous things
about you, Nina Dewdrop."

Chapter Four

Nina was desperate to tell Peri and Bella all about her conversation with Miss Bliss. She caught them in the corridor before the day's classes began and hurriedly filled them in on what she'd just seen and heard.

"Wow, what a story," said Bella, shaking her head.

"I know," said Nina. "No wonder she didn't want to tell the whole class. It's so sad! What do you reckon, Peri?"

"Sounds like she made the right choice to me," Peri answered carelessly.

"What?" cried Bella. "You must be mad! If I ever get a job in the Royal Fairy Ballet, I'll *never* give it up!"

Peri suddenly looked cross and shouted, "You think you've got all the answers, don't you, Bella Glove? Well maybe being a professional ballerina isn't the be-all and end-all for everyone!"

She flew off to class in a huff, leaving her stunned friends to follow in silence.

The fairies didn't have a chance to chat to Peri again, as Miss Bliss was keen to start lessons.

"To work, fairies!" she cried as the ballerinas took their places in the studio. "We're going to do some more on *The Nutcracker* today to get you in the mood for our trip! Nina, I know you've found out about the story – can you tell the class a bit of it?" she asked.

"It's quite a tricky story," Nina said cautiously. "I'm not sure I'll be able to remember it all . . . Let's see . . . It starts on Christmas Eve. A family called the Stahlbaums is throwing a party, and the children, Clara and Fritz, are very excited because their godfather, Herr Drosselmeyer, is coming." Nina looked at Miss Bliss for reassurance.

"That's right," said Miss Bliss. "He is a toy-maker and a magician. Once upon a time he worked in the royal palace, where he invented a mousetrap that killed off most of the mice. In revenge the wicked Queen of the Mice cast a horrid spell on Herr Drosselmeyer's handsome nephew, Hans-Peter, and turned him into an ugly nutcracker doll."

"Oh yes! I remember − Clara's godfather gives her the nutcracker as a present, doesn't he?" said Nina.

"Yes, because her godfather knows that only Clara can turn the nutcracker back into Hans-Peter. The nutcracker needs a young girl to love him and care for him, even though he is ugly. She must help him kill the Mouse King, so that he can turn into a handsome young man again . . ."

"Sounds bonkers," cut in Peri. "It'd make a silly play."

What's got into her? thought Nina. She's in a real mood.

Miss Bliss laughed. "I agree, it is a bit strange, Peri, and it probably wouldn't work well as a play or a storybook, but it's a fabulous ballet, believe me."

Peri shuffled her feet awkwardly.

"What happens next, Miss?" asked Nyssa Bean.

"I'll show you!" said Miss Bliss. "Stand back."

The pretty teacher held her silver wand high in the air and cried:

Take us now to the Land of Snow,
Where Hans-Peter and Clara go
To see the snowflakes whirl and dance,

Their white dresses shimmering as they prance,
Then on to the Land of Sweets,
Here there's a garden made of treats,
Where the Sugar Plum Fairy and her Prince
Have lived together ever since . . .

The Second Years drew back as the
studio was suddenly filled with a blizzard
of dazzling snowflakes, swirling in eddies
from the ceiling. As the snowstorm began
to fade, Nina could just make out some
tiny figures dancing in mid-air. She
gasped as she realized that she was
watching miniature fairies, performing
the waltz called the "Dance of the
Snowflakes". As soon as this dance
ended, a river appeared on the studio
floor – but it was not an ordinary river.
It was flowing with clear, sparkling
lemonade! The banks of the river were
clustered with jewel-like flowers made
from sweets, and a magical castle of
caramels, marzipan, gingerbread and

peppermints appeared before the fairies'
eyes.

"This is the Land of Sweets, where
Clara sees the Sugar Plum Fairy dance
with her Prince," said Miss Bliss. She

✿ ✿ ✿ **27** ✿ ✿ ✿

waved her wand once again, and the scene vanished.

The Second Years cried out, "Oh, Miss! Show us more, please!"

Miss Bliss smiled. "No," she said. "We must do some work now! In any case, I don't want to spoil the show for you – you must wait until we get to Clover Garden to see the rest."

Bella turned to Peri and whispered, "Still think it's bonkers?"

But Peri just shrugged and turned away.

Chapter Five

The Second-Year ballerinas spent the rest of term working hard on improvisation based on the story of *The Nutcracker*, and learning new moves in their demi-pointe shoes. Outside in the field, the wild flowers had died, the leaves had fallen from the big oak tree that housed the Academy, and the fairies awoke each morning to frosted windows. They wondered if it might snow. Nina and Bella threw themselves into the classes with enthusiasm. Their new teacher made everything such fun, and her love of *The*

Nutcracker made the fairies all the more excited about the forthcoming trip. Nina did notice that Peri wasn't as keen on lessons as the other fairy ballerinas, but whenever she tried to talk to her friend about it, Peri always had an excuse: she was tired; she couldn't learn the new steps; she was just daydreaming. Nina didn't believe any of the excuses, but gave up trying to get to the bottom of her friend's moods, telling herself that once Peri saw the Royal Fairy Ballet perform, she would brighten up.

The day before the trip, Miss Bliss told the class some more about the "Dance of the Sugar Plum Fairy" – her favourite part.

"The correct ballet term for the dance is a 'pas de deux'," Miss Bliss explained. "That means it is a dance for two people, and it is usually between a man and a woman. It's a shame there are no boys at the Academy . . . oh well, I suppose we

can pair you up and have a go anyway!
Nina, come to the front, please. And, er,
let's see . . . Nyssa, you too."

Miss Bliss gently moved Nyssa to stand
behind Nina.

"I'm going to take you through what
is known as an 'enchaînement'," she said.
"That means a sequence of movements –
like a little routine," she explained. "Now,
Nina, please will you do a 'tendu croisé
derrière' on demi-pointe
with your arms in
second position."

Nina gracefully
held her arms out
to the sides in
second position.
She turned her
head elegantly to the
left and stretched

her left leg out behind her with her toe
pointed neatly. Her right leg was turned
out beautifully with her foot at right
angles to her hips.

"That is magnificent, Nina!" Miss Bliss
cried. "Now, Nyssa, you are the 'man'
today."

Some of the ballerinas started tittering.

"Shh! Don't be silly, class. What I am
asking Nyssa to do is very difficult, so
she needs to concentrate," said Miss Bliss
seriously.

"Too right it's difficult," muttered Peri.
"Miss Tremula never asked us to turn into
men!"

Bella stifled a giggle.

Miss Bliss turned her attention back
to Nyssa. "The most important thing to
know about a pas de deux is that the
man and woman must match each other
exactly. This means that when Nina
moves, Nyssa must move. It must look
as if they are attached to each other by

invisible threads. So, Nyssa, try to copy Nina's 'attitude' exactly please."

Nyssa held her arms out in second position just like Nina and stretched her left leg behind her, pointing her toe. Her right leg was lovely and strong, and her foot was turned out just like Nina's.

"That's wonderful!" their teacher cried. "But, Nyssa, make sure your head is facing in exactly the same direction as Nina's – that's it, lovely long necks. And, Nyssa, you need to place your left hand gently round Nina's waist. Right, now comes the tricky bit. You must both move into a small waltz step at *exactly* the same time, like this." Miss Bliss demonstrated the movement she wanted by starting in a tendu croisé derrière. She gracefully drew her left foot in behind her right so that it was pointed and just touching the back of her right foot, which was still turned out. At the same time, she turned her head gently to the left and placed her arms in fourth position, looking down at her left hand.

The class held its breath as Nina and Nyssa tried to move together. It started well – they both managed to bring their left foot neatly in behind their right – but when Nyssa turned her head to look down at her left hand, which was still on Nina's waist, she lost her balance,

wobbled and leaned too heavily on her friend. The two ballerinas fell forward and landed in a giggling heap.

"It's harder than you'd think, isn't it?" said their teacher, laughing. "Remember that, when you watch the Sugar Plum Fairy and her Prince dancing together tomorrow at the Opera House . . ."

Chapter Six

A fleet of dragonflies took the fairies to Clover Garden. They hummed and whirred as they hovered over the Garden, which was a hive of activity, with dragonflies from all over fairyland taking off and landing every second. Nina felt dazed by the level of noise and the crowds of other fairies. She was not used to big cities. Everywhere she looked there were fairies performing street theatre, busking or doing circus acts. Nina got the fright of her life when they flew past what she thought was a golden statue of

Cinderella's fairy godmother and it sprang suddenly to life, crying, "Don't forget, Cinderella – you must come home on the stroke of midnight!"

Bella creased up laughing at the look of horror on Nina's face. "It's just an actor painted gold, silly! I think it's wicked!"

"Yeah!" Nina breathed. She was lost for words. Hornbeamster, the town where the Academy was, was not as exciting as this.

"Mum's always coming here," said Bella, raising her eyebrows. "She witters on about the 'darling' boutiques and cafes." Bella's mum, Foxy Glove, was a famous jazz dancer who socialized with all the stars of fairyland and was frequently out and about at celebrity events. Bella found the whole thing incredibly embarrassing.

"You have to admit, it's *so* cool to be here," Nina said. "Isn't it, Peri?"

But Peri was already fluttering away from her friends, waving happily at someone in the crowd. Nina was sure she recognized the figure from their summer holidays: it was Willow Shakespindle, the famous fairy playwright.

"I'm just going to say hi, Nina!" Peri called. "I'll catch you up later."

Oh, I hope Peri doesn't get lost. I'd better not tell Miss Bliss . . .

"Fairies!" the teacher was calling to the class. "This is the Royal Fairy Opera House!" The teacher pointed her wand to her right and an arc of rainbow glitter shot out in a large arrow that pointed to a huge white building ringed with imposing columns and marble statues of famous fairy opera singers and ballerinas. Miss Bliss asked the fairies to line up outside the decorated glass doors. "I've got a special surprise for you, fairies," the teacher announced, beaming. "I had a chat with an old friend and he's agreed to

give you a guided tour of the Royal Fairy
Opera House before the show starts! I'll
just let him know we're all here."

Nina was about to tell Miss Bliss that
Peri wasn't with the group, when her
spiky-haired friend appeared suddenly at
her side. Her emerald eyes were gleaming
and she looked happier than she had for
ages.

"It's fab here, isn't it?" she whispered
to Nina.

"Yes," Nina replied slowly. "Peri,
what were you talking to Willow about?"

"Shh, you two!" hissed Bella. "Miss
Bliss is back — and look at the fairy she's
got with her. He is gorgeous!"

"Oh, pack it in, Bella," Nina
began, but then she turned to look at
the newcomer and gasped. He was
breathtakingly handsome — he looked like
a fairy prince! His hair was golden blond
and his blue eyes shone like sapphires.

"This is Rowan Larch," said Miss Bliss,

smiling. "Rowan is dancing the role of the Sugar Plum Prince later this evening, but he has kindly agreed to show us around first."

"It will be my pleasure, Petunia," said Rowan in a deep, smooth voice. "It's wonderful to see you again."

Nina looked at her teacher – she could have sworn that Miss Bliss was fluttering her wings and blushing.

Chapter Seven

Rowan kept the Second Years spellbound with tales of working for the Royal Fairy Ballet as he swept up the wide silver staircase that led from the foyer to the seating area and all the backstage rooms.

He hovered outside a door that was covered in thick purple velvet with tiny silver stars embroidered all over it. On a silver plaque in the middle of the door, the name "Rowan Larch" was written in extravagant silver letters.

"This is my dressing room," Rowan

said, rather unnecessarily. "Petunia said you would like to see where we get changed and so on – is that right?"

"Oh yes, absolutely!" gushed Bella, wriggling nearer the front of the group so that she could get closer to Rowan. Nina rolled her eyes.

"We rehearse rigorously of course, but in the afternoon before we perform, we have to rest our muscles," he was saying. "I am very fortunate as I have a cosy dressing room, so I can shut myself away in here and relax."

"Cosy" was not the word Nina would have chosen for the room. It was magnificently luxurious! There was a huge mirror at one end, lit up by dozens and dozens of tiny fireflies around its rim. In front of the mirror was a silver table covered in various brushes and hundreds of tiny pots, which were his make-up for the show.

In front of the table was a soft velvet seat in the shape of a heart. It was the same purple as the dressing-room door and was also covered in hundreds of tiny silver stars.

"This is where my costume is brought to me once it has been ironed and any necessary repairs have been made,"

Rowan explained. "We are very lucky to have a great team of dressmakers here, and they work extremely quickly," he added.

Nina thought back to her visit to the Fairy Palace, when she had put on a show there with Peri and Bella. They had met the royal dressmaker, Juniper Bindweed, who had made the most elaborate costumes for them.

Nina stared in awe at the rack of jewel-encrusted outfits that shimmered and glinted in the light of the fireflies.

Rowan took them out into the corridor again and told them they could see where the costumes were made. They flew round the glistening circular corridors until eventually they stopped outside a plain white door. Nina thought she could make out the sound of whirring and clicking.

Rowan opened the door cautiously and there was a great flapping of wings and some squeaking, then silence. The Second

Years peered in — the room was empty, save for row upon row of golden sewing machines. The workstations seemed to have been abandoned in a hurry, as there were piles of fabric and half-finished costumes everywhere.

"It's all right — it's just our visitors!" Rowan called out in his deep, soothing voice.

With a flurry and flutter, a host of tiny fairies buzzed out of hiding like a swarm of silver bees. They shyly flew back to their workstations without a glance at the ballerinas and resumed their sewing.

"I'm sorry about that," said Rowan. "Our dressmakers are not used to company and like to be left in peace when they work. We'll leave you now — thank you so much!" he called, and gently shut the door.

What a magical place! thought Nina. She couldn't wait to see the show.

Chapter Eight

The time had come to take their seats for the performance. The class was shown to their places in the stalls by a pretty fairy dressed in a white leotard and silver tutu. She handed out some programmes that listed the names of all the dancers and explained the story of *The Nutcracker*.

If they had been impressed by the rooms backstage at the Opera House, the ballerinas were blown away by the main auditorium. The stage was huge. There were heavy, dark red velvet curtains

edged with gold across the front of the
stage, and the stalls, boxes and circle were
lit by rows and rows of glimmering
fireflies. The seats were the same deep red
velvet as the stage curtains and, when
Nina looked up, she saw a massive
chandelier made of frozen water droplets,
lit by a swarm of fireflies.

"How does the water stay frozen and
not melt?" she wondered aloud.

"Magic, darling," said the white and
silver fairy. "Pure magic."

Nina and her friends filed down the
row of seats that had been reserved for
them and sank into the plush velvet with
a sigh. She looked up at the ornate ceiling
decorated with elegant dancing fairies,
and then scanned the boxes until she
realized she was looking at the Royal Box
– and there was someone she recognized.
Waving at her!

It was Princess Coriander. She flicked
her wand quickly and a piece of paper

landed on Nina's lap. It was a note from
the cheeky princess:

Come to a party backstage
after the performance!
Love C x

Nina beamed and waved back at the
princess to show she'd got the message. At
that moment, the orchestra struck up the
opening bars of *The Nutcracker*. The heavy
red curtains swept back from the stage to
reveal the Stahlbaums' luxurious living
room.

It looks so real! Nina thought.

She felt as if she was actually there in
the house with the children, Clara and
Fritz. There was a huge Christmas tree
in the centre at the back of the stage,
glistening with lights and candles and
tiny glass decorations; pictures were hung
on the walls and there was a chandelier
hanging from the ceiling, much like the

one above the audience in the Opera House.

The ballet began. The Stahlbaums danced around each other in circles, busying themselves with preparations for their Christmas party. Then the imposing figure of Herr Drosselmeyer, the children's godfather, appeared. The programme notes explained that Herr Drosselmeyer was what was called a "character part". Nina glanced through the notes to find out more. The notes said:

A "character" is more like an actor than a dancer. These parts are usually played by older dancers who are no longer young and supple enough to dance in the corps de ballet or as a soloist.

Nina looked back up at the stage and watched in awe as the scene changed magically before her eyes. Clara had come downstairs to check on the broken nutcracker doll, and was now shrinking to the size of a doll herself, or so it seemed . . . then Nina realized that what was really happening was that the set was getting larger! The Christmas tree was growing and growing and all the toys in the nursery were getting bigger and bigger. Clara now looked as though she was the same size as the nutcracker doll, and he himself had come to life!

Chapter Nine

At last, Clara broke the wicked spell that had changed Herr Drosselmeyer's nephew into the nutcracker so long ago, and the ugly little wooden doll was suddenly transformed into the handsome young man called Hans-Peter. The happy couple whirled and twirled together with joy and found themselves magically transported to the Land of Snow, where they were caught in a beautiful blizzard by the "Dance of the Snowflakes". Ballerinas dressed in shimmering white and silver costumes whizzed around the stage.

The scenery changed again to a
magical world, where all the buildings
and the flowers and trees were made
of pink, lilac and lime-green sweets,
glistening with icing sugar. This was Miss
Bliss's favourite part: the "Dance of the
Sugar Plum Fairy" in the Sugar Garden
in the Land of Sweets.

"There's Rowan!" Bella hissed,
bringing Nina back down to earth for a
moment. "Doesn't he look fantastic?"

His costume could have been made
from real sweets for all Nina knew.
He was dressed from head to toe in
glimmering white with frostings of pink
and gold on his tunic.

Miss Bliss leaned down the row and
whispered to her pupils: "This is the part
where Hans-Peter uses mime — watch
carefully!"

Hans-Peter mimed how Clara had
saved him and broken the spell. He let
his arm drop down limply as if he was

still a doll, then he mimed how Clara
had thrown her shoe at the Mouse King.
Finally he pretended to be the dead king.
Nina was amazed at how she knew

exactly what the dancer was "saying", even though he wasn't using words.

Then the Sugar Plum Fairy and her Prince danced for Clara and Hans-Peter. They performed a dazzling pas de deux to silvery notes played on glockenspiel and strings. Clarinets sang out a gentle tune as the Fairy and her Prince mirrored each other's moves perfectly.

Nina glanced down the row at Miss Bliss. The pretty teacher was entranced as she watched Rowan dance.

She looks as if she wishes she were the Sugar Plum Fairy herself! thought Nina.

All too soon the ballet moved on to the last dance – the "Waltz of the Flowers", which Miss Bliss had performed earlier in the term when Nina had disturbed her.

The ballet ended with Clara back in her house on Christmas morning, wondering if her adventure had been a dream. She rushed out into the

street through the snow to try to find
her godfather and tell him what had
happened. But on the way she bumped
into a young man who looked exactly
like Hans-Peter . . .

Nina felt that she too must have
been dreaming, when the Opera House
lights came on and the curtains fell on
the stage. She blinked and rubbed her
eyes in the bright lights, overwhelmed
by the experience. With a loud whirring
of wings, the audience in the Opera
House rose from their seats clapping.
The applause seemed to be never-ending.
Nina hoped that if they clapped hard
enough, they might be able to convince
the dancers to perform the ballet all over
again. But finally the applause faded
and gave way to a buzz of chatter and
laughter as the audience began to flutter
out of the rows of seats and leave the
auditorium.

Nina was still hovering above her

seat, staring dreamily at the stage, lost in
The Nutcracker's magical world. She was
reliving the story, putting herself in the
place of Clara, imagining what it would
be like to leap across the stage of the
Royal Fairy Opera House . . . she was
dimly aware of someone talking to her
and snapped back
to reality as she
realized that all
her friends had
left her and
were filing out
of their row.

"Follow me,
fairies," Miss Bliss was
saying. "Nina! The
ballet's finished,
dear."

Nina's face
fell. She did not want
her dream treat to
be over so soon.

Then she remembered Princess Coriander's invitation. She cheered up at the thought of meeting her cheeky friend again.

"Miss Bliss, can we go to the party backstage?" she asked, showing her teacher the note.

Miss Bliss smiled. "Of course! I was going

to take you anyway. Rowan had already invited us."

"Cool," said Bella. "We love a party, don't we, Peri?"

But Peri didn't answer. She had vanished again.

Chapter Ten

Backstage was a riot of noise and laughter when Nina and Bella arrived. The rest of the Second Years were already enjoying themselves, chatting to the members of the Royal Fairy Ballet and asking for autographs and photos. Nina and Bella had tried to find Peri in the auditorium but had given up, deciding that she must have gone on ahead to the party. But they couldn't see her with the other Second Years. Nina spotted Rowan though. He was holding hands with Miss Bliss!

"Hi, guys!" Princess Coriander whizzed over, her tiara slightly askew. "I'm so glad you've come. These parties are so boring."

"Hi, Coriander," said Nina. "Sorry we're a bit late. We were looking for Peri. She keeps disappearing. Have you seen her?"

"Peri? Oh, yeah, she's over there talking to Willow Shakespindle – you know, the acting guy," Coriander said.

Queen Camellia gracefully fluttered over.

"Darling, I do wish you would speak more like a princess," she said wearily.

Coriander sighed loudly and ignored her mother. "Whatever! Don't worry about Peri," she said to Nina. "She looks happy enough to me. Anyway, listen to this – I've got some great news! In fact, I want to tell Peri too. Hang on, I'll just get her . . ."

As soon as Coriander came back over with Peri, Nina grabbed her friend's arm.

"Where have you been? Why do you

keep flying off? Are you all right?" she
said in a rush.

"Calm down!" said Peri, laughing.
"I've been with Willow. He brought some
of his pupils from the stage school to see
the ballet. Holly Nightshade's twin, Polly,
is here too. It's been a blast seeing her
again— –"

Nina cut in impatiently. "You could
have told us where you'd gone, Peri," she
snapped.

The bright smile faded from Peri's lips
and she stared at the floor.

"What is it?" Nina asked, suddenly
feeling worried. Why *was* her friend
behaving so strangely?

"The thing is, I've been doing a lot
of thinking recently, and I've . . . well,
I've sort of come to a decision," Peri said
quietly.

Nina felt her stomach lurch.

"You're making me nervous, Peri," she
said urgently. "*Please* tell me what's up."

Peri took a deep breath, fixed her friend in the eye and said firmly, "I'm going to leave the Academy, Nina."

"Oh!" Nina cried, her hands flying to her mouth in horror. "No! No, Peri, you can't leave!" she cried. "I *knew* you were upset about something – I should have tried to help you! This is all my fault—"

"No, it's not," said Peri kindly. "I'm sorry, Nina. I've dreaded telling you. I knew you would try to talk me out of it, but I am absolutely sure that this is the right thing to do."

Nina grabbed Bella now. "Did you know about this?" she asked her.

Bella was looking stunned. She dumbly shook her head as a tear rolled down her cheek.

"What are you going to do, Peri?" Nina asked shakily. "Are you going back to your granny's?"

"No," she said. She took another deep breath. "Nina, you know that I'm not the greatest fairy ballerina – no, it's true," she said as her friend started to protest. "I only got a place at the Academy because Granny had been a pupil there. But, apart from being friends with you and Bella, there is nothing I enjoy about the Academy. I thought I could stick it out because of you two," she said, smiling weakly, "but I'm afraid the lessons are still torture. When I met Willow at the Festival of Fairy Arts last summer, I realized there was something else I could do that I was really good at, and ever since then I haven't been able to stop thinking about becoming an actor. I kept in touch with Willow and spent all my spare time reading plays, but I thought I had to stick it out as a ballerina. Then you told me what Miss Bliss said about knowing when the time has come to give up."

Nina was crying now. "I wish I'd never told you that!" she shouted. "Oh, Peri, please don't go!"

Peri shook her head and started to cry herself. "Miss Bliss was right. You have to know when to give up. I've always known that I will never be a great ballerina – not like you, Nina. But I think I *could* make it as an actor . . . I will miss you guys so much, but Willow

has offered me a place at his stage school.
This is my big chance, guys. I hope you'll
understand. And don't worry," she added,
flinging her arms around her two best
friends. "I'll stay in touch! You can come
and visit me any time you like!"

Nina nodded through her tears as
Bella held on to Peri tightly.

"Ahem," said a small voice.

The three sad fairy friends pulled away
from each other and wiped their eyes.
Princess Coriander was trying to get their
attention. They had forgotten about her.

"I'm really sorry about you going,
Peri," she said quietly.

Peri smiled. "Thanks, Coriander," she
said.

"It's just that . . . I would have liked
to have got to know you better," said the
little princess.

"Oh? How's that?" Peri asked, puzzled.

"Well," Coriander began shyly. "I,
er . . . oh, forget it, maybe now's not the

best time to tell you," she said, turning to leave.

"Coriander! You can't leave us in suspense!" Nina cried.

The princess turned back to face the three friends, a huge grin on her face, and said, "I've got a place at the Royal Academy of Fairy Ballet – and I'm starting next term!"

Nina and Bella zoomed up into the air with joy and whooped, "Yay! Fantastic!"

Peri hugged the fairy princess. "That's fab, Coriander. Well, now you know I'm leaving, I expect you to take great care of my two best friends!"

Coriander hugged Peri back and grabbed Nina and Bella and hugged them tightly as well. "You bet I will!" she cried.

Fairy Stories

Chosen by Anna Wilson

Every fairy has a story to tell

Be spirited away to fairyland and visit the wonderful worlds of dream fairies, funny fairy godmothers, a sweet-toothed cake fairy and a fairy who learns a lot about friendship.

This magical story collection is a must for all fairy fans.

Log on to

Nina
Fairy Ballerina
.com

for magical games, activities and fun!

Experience the magical world of Nina and her friends at the Royal Academy of Fairy Ballet. There are games to play, fun activities to make or do, plus you can learn more about the Nina Fairy Ballerina books!

Log on to www.ninafairyballerina.com now!

A selected list of titles available from Macmillan Children's Books

The prices shown below are correct at the time of going to press. However, Macmillan Publishers reserves the right to show new retail prices on covers, which may differ from those previously advertised.

ANNA WILSON

NINA FAIRY BALLERINA

New Girl	978-0-330-43985-5	£3.99
Daisy Shoes	978-0-330-43986-2	£3.99
Best Friends	978-0-330-43987-9	£3.99
Show Time	978-0-330-43988-6	£3.99
Flying Colours	978-0-330-44622-8	£3.99
Double Trouble	978-0-330-44620-4	£3.99
Party Magic	978-0-330-44778-2	£3.99
Dream Treat	978-0-330-44780-5	£3.99
FAIRY STORIES	978-0-330-43823-9	£4.99

All Pan Macmillan titles can be ordered from our website, www.panmacmillan.com, or from your local bookshop and are also available by post from:

Bookpost, PO Box 29, Douglas, Isle of Man IM99 1BQ
Credit cards accepted. For details:
Telephone: 01624 677237
Fax: 01624 670923
Email: bookshop@enterprise.net
www.bookpost.co.uk

Free postage and packing in the United Kingdom